To MARCUS

Merry Christmas!

Keith Turner
12/3/87

To Brittney, CASSANDRA, Amelia and Brandon

May the Joy of
Christmas remain with
you always!

KH Turner
2007

The Magic Kriss Karpet

Written by K. K. Corner
Illustrated by Sharon L. Richert

RENROC INCORPORATED, PUBLISHERS
SEATTLE, WASHINGTON

FIRST EDITION
Text and Illustrations
Copyright © 1987 by K. K. Corner

ISBN: 0-932197-03-5

Library of Congress Catalog Card Number 87-61145
The Magic Kriss Karpet™ and Sir Jeffery™
are licensed trademarks of Renroc, Inc.

To my children—
Kevin, Candace
and Cynthia

There once was a little boy named Brian who lived in a cozy house on the snowy and wintery edges of the midnight sun.

Brian's bedroom was exactly one horizon away from the North Pole. Outside his home was a large wooden sign which read: "NORTH POLE-THREE CHIMNEYS-TWO JUMPS-ONE SKIP AWAY".

Brian was indeed a very fortunate boy. His home was Santa's FIRST STOP on Christmas Eve. He lived nearer to Santa's northern hideaway than did any other child in the entire world.

AND EVERY YEAR, TWO NIGHTS BEFORE
CHRISTMAS . . .

Santa's elves would warm up the restless reindeer in high-flying circles above the nearby housetops. Over and over again, the light-footed runners loved to land and skitter — prancing and dancing — on Brian's roof. Brian would hear the WHOOSH of their hoofs as they flew overhead, but he was never quite fast enough to see their sparkle in the sky. By the time the little boy jumped out of bed and ran to the window, the swift sky riders had vanished into the frigid night.

For the past two years, Brian had been nimble enough to climb upon the slippery roof and soon discovered, to his amazement, glistening strands of reindeer hair lying in the snow around the chimney. He had carefully rolled and folded each shiny fiber into a large MATCHBOX which he kept under his pillow.

The matchbox contained, of course, this special secret — only Brian and his dog, Sir Jeffery, knew of it!

NOW ON *THIS* CHRISTMAS EVE . . .

Brian was almost asleep when a strange gleam suddenly appeared from the matchbox beneath his pillow. Lifting the pillow, he reached for the glimmering box, but it slipped through his fingers and began SOARING and SWOOPING wildly around the bedroom. Sir Jeffery jumped off the bed, barking excitedly.

Brian leaped high and caught the spinning carton, but was whisked about like a feather in a whirlwind until he and the box softly landed in a heap on the foot of his bed.

He rubbed his eyes in disbelief.

"Did you see that, Sir Jeffery? I just flew around the room!" he exclaimed.

Although the hour was late, Brian was now wide-awake. He quickly put on his pants, sweater and snow boots and tiptoed into the sewing room by his bedroom where he took a large darning needle from his mother's sewing basket.

Tiptoeing back into his bedroom, Brian sat down by Sir Jeffery, who had jumped back on the bed.

He lifted the bright tufts of reindeer hair from the matchbox and used the needle to begin weaving each willowy strand between the folds of a scatter rug which he had picked up from the floor by his bed.

Pulling the rug up onto his lap, Brian leaned over and whispered to his dog, ''Maybe . . . I sure hope . . . maybe my scatter rug will fly, too!''

He had just finished sewing the last hair into the small carpet when suddenly it twisted out of his fingers, spiralled upward towards the ceiling, then hung suspended in the Christmas air like a shimmering space ship.

Brian shinnied easily up the rug's ribbons of color, squeezing his legs and snow boots into the soft yarn, and knelt down on the carpet.

"Come on, Sir Jeffery," the little boy called to his faithful dog. "Jump on! This is fun!" But Sir Jeffery didn't budge! He just wagged his short tail, barked nervously, and blinked his eyes, which were almost hidden under a crop of black, wiry hair.

All of a sudden a tinkling voice sounded from the carpet, saying:

"A Magic Carpet now am I;
You've given me the will to fly;
Now your servant I will be . . .
Incline your ear and hear my plea:

"Speak to me in total rhyme
And only then at Christmas time;
My magic spell shall thus be borne
From Christmas Eve till Christmas Morn.

"Power to soar like graceful birds,
Command me with these magic words:
'Spinsel Low, Spinsel High,
Kriss Karpet to the sky!' "

Whereupon the rug and its youthful rider floated gently down onto the bedroom floor.

"Whew! Wow!" exclaimed Brian breathlessly. "Did you hear that, Sir Jeffery? Did you hear the Kriss Karpet's 'magic words'?"

The little boy picked up his dog and lovingly held him in his arms. Sir Jeffery was very old, you see, and nearly blind in both eyes.

"This is Christmas Eve!" Brian announced. "We can FLY tonight! The Kriss Karpet has promised to take us *anywhere* — tonight!"

Brian's eyes sparkled as he looked out his bedroom window at the twinkling stars.

"I know!" he said in a hushed tone. "Let's find a pair of *glasses* for you this Christmas . . . glasses to help you *see.*" Sir Jeffery wagged his tail, and licked his master's face. Jumping down from Brian's arms, he danced around the room.

Brian waited until he was sure his parents were sound asleep. He unrolled the Kriss Karpet in the middle of his room and motioned for Sir Jeffery to sit beside him on the colorful rug.

Holding the little dog tightly, Brian commanded the carpet:

"Spinsel Low, Spinsel High,
Kriss Karpet to the sky!
Fly us quickly — do not dally —
To the place called 'Spectacle Valley'!"

Out the window they flew . . . higher . . . faster . . . farther . . . then lower . . . slower . . . until the Kriss Karpet glided down and came to rest in a glittering land filled with all manner of wonderful sights: milk shake fountains, candy cane mountains; root beer waterfalls, malted milk balls; jellybean trees, bubble gum leaves; paths with ice cream edges bordered by gumdrop hedges.

As Brian looked around in wonderment, he spied a sign which read: "THIS WAY TO THE VALLEY OF SPECTACLES". He tucked the Kriss Karpet under his arm, turned to Sir Jeffery, and said excitedly, "Come on — let's follow it!"

As they skipped along the path, Brian eagerly pulled the gumdrops from the hedges, and stuffed his mouth and pockets with jellybeans and bubble gum from the trees. He stopped often to drink from the many milk shake fountains.

Before long the path forked. The sign on the right read "SPECTACLE VALLEY". The one on the left pointed to "PIRATE'S GOLD CREEK".

"Pirate's Gold!" Brian exclaimed. "I wonder if it's real gold? Let's find out!"

Brian and Sir Jeffery followed the left fork until they came to a creek sparkling with all the colors of the rainbow. Along its banks were thousands of gold coins and nuggets! The little boy hurriedly emptied his pockets of all the jellybeans and bubble gum, then filled them with the bright yellow nuggets until they bulged at the seams.

"This is the best Christmas ever! I've found the Pirate's Lost Treasure!" Brian sang heartily, as he and Sir Jeffery turned and ran back to the sign which read: "SPECTACLE VALLEY".

The small boy had not forgotten his Christmas promise to his beloved dog. "We've got to find those glasses for you, Sir Jeffery," he said. "Let's go to Spectacle Valley!"

Brian glanced at the horizon. It was nearly daybreak. He remembered the Kriss Karpet's words:

"My magic spell shall thus be borne
From Christmas Eve till Christmas Morn."

"We'll have to hurry," Brian urged. "The Karpet's spell ends at sunrise. Run fast or we'll never make it back home."

The two adventurers scurried along the trail, not even taking time to nibble at the ice cream along its edges.

"Whoa!" gasped Brian as they rounded a bend and almost ran into a strange-looking man.

Short and stout, with long white hair and mustache, wearing a purple and green coat and top hat, the strange man stood right in the middle of the path, blocking their way.

"Who . . . who are y-you?" stammered Brian.

The short man peered through his magnifying glass at the two small travelers.

"I'm Mister Eye-Catcher," he answered pompously. "I'm the keeper of the gate to the Valley of Spectacles," he continued as he pointed to a curved gate farther down the trail. "Which one of you needs a pair of glasses?"

"Can we *really* get glasses *here*?" Brian asked hopefully.

The gatekeeper laughed while he studied his two guests through his monocle. "You bet your eye you can!" he answered. "We've got nothing *but* spectacles in this valley. Who needs some eyeglasses?"

Brian jumped up and down and shouted the answer loudly. "*Sir Jeffery* needs glasses! *That's* why we're here — to find glasses for him!"

"Then follow me!" commanded Mr. Eye-Catcher.

The portly man led the way down the path and through the gate into the valley beyond.

Soon they entered a beautiful forest of strange and wonderful trees: trees with thousands of colorful eyeglasses hanging from their branches. Blue glasses, yellow glasses, red and green eyepieces, purple monocles — every color imaginable.

All the trees were carefully marked with bright signs below their branches which read: ''Cat Glasses'', ''Bat Glasses'', ''Owl Glasses'', ''Fowl Glasses'', ''Dog Glasses'', ''Frog Glasses'', ''Moose Glasses'', ''Goose Glasses''.

There were ''Mouse Glasses'', ''Dodo Glasses'', ''Donkey Glasses'' and ''Dragon Glasses''. Even spectacle trees for turtles, toucans and teddy bears, elephants, giraffes, butterflies and hummingbirds.

Mr. Eye-Catcher reached high and shook the limbs of the ''Dog Glasses'' tree. Six pairs of spectacles, each a different color, fell to the ground.

Brian tried a pair of the glasses on Sir Jeffery. They fit perfectly! Sir Jeffery wagged his tail — he could see!

''Oh, thanks loads! Thanks a million!'' gushed Brian.

"Wait a minute . . . just a minute," called the Catcher. "They are *not* free!"

"But I don't have any money," pleaded Brian.

"What do you have in *there?*" asked the short man as he peered through his magnifying glass at Brian's bulging pockets.

"Oh, those are my nuggets from Pirate's Gold Creek," said the little boy proudly.

"Give them to me!" demanded the gatekeeper.

"*All* of them? Every last *one?*" cried Brian, tears brimming his eyes.

"Yes! All of them! Empty your pockets," Mr. Eye-Catcher replied firmly.

"But I want to take them home with me. They're from the 'Pirate's Lost Treasure'," responded Brian glumly.

"It's either the gold or the glasses. You can't have them both," argued the Catcher.

Brian hesitated. He reached into one of his pockets, removed some of the yellow nuggets and rolled them over and over in his hands.

The little boy turned around slowly and watched as Sir Jeffery danced joyfully under the "Dog Glasses" tree.

"Well? What shall it be?" prompted the round man.

"My dog *really* needs those glasses," Brian answered earnestly. "I'll trade you, then. I'll give you my gold for those six pairs of glasses."

He reached in his pockets, took out all the glittering stones and handed them to Mr. Eye-Catcher.

The little traveler glanced at the horizon. It was beginning to get light! He quickly unrolled the Kriss Karpet and beckoned to his dog. "Hurry, Sir Jeffery! Jump on! It's time to go!"

Gathering up the lenses, he waved to the gatekeeper, who was peering at Brian through his monocle. "Goodbye, Mr. Eye-Catcher. Thanks for the glasses. We'll see you next Christmas."

With a youthful shout he gave the magic command:

"Spinsel Low, Spinsel High,
Kriss Karpet to the Sky!
With these words here's my rhyme,
Take us home 'in the nick of time.' "

The Kriss Karpet flew much higher and faster on the way back home. The colorful dog glasses fell out of Brian's pocket and were blowing away in the rush of the wind. The small boy grabbed the last pair, which were bright yellow, and held onto them tightly.

Before long the carpet glided into Brian's bedroom just as the sun's rays streamed over the horizon. Brian and Sir Jeffery were both very tired and fell asleep on the Kriss Karpet as soon as it touched down on the bedroom floor. . . .

LATER THAT MORNING . . .

"Merry Christmas," sang Brian's mother cheerfully as she entered his room. Brian was not in his bed. "Why are you sleeping on the floor?" she asked curiously.

Brian rubbed his eyes, yawned and glanced around the room. Then he remembered!

"Mother," he asked, "where are the yellow dog glasses?"

"What on earth are you talking about? What yellow dog glasses?" asked his mother.

"Sir Jeffery's glasses," Brian answered. The little boy jumped up from the floor and dashed into the living room where, nestled among the Christmas tree ornaments, lay a pair of bright, yellow glasses.

Brian held them up for his mother to see. "Here they are! These are my dog's glasses," he said gleefully.

He called his pet and placed the yellow rims on Sir Jeffery's nose and over his pointed ears. They fit perfectly, of course.

"Where did those come from, Brian?" asked his mother. She was puzzled . . . they weren't there on Christmas Eve. She had put the finishing touches to the tree and certainly would have remembered seeing them.

"Ah, um, out there," Brian answered vaguely. "I mean . . . uh . . . I got them from Mr. Eye-Catcher at the 'Valley of Spectacles'. Sir Jeffery and I flew there. Last night!"

"You flew *where? When?*" his mother quizzed.

"To 'Spectacle Valley', and 'Pirate's Gold Creek', last night, and I got lots of gold and traded it for six pairs of glasses, but lost five, and almost ran out of time, and just made it home," Brian rambled.

His mother smiled. "You and your imagination," she teased. Then she leaned over and gave Brian a big kiss.

"I'm starting Christmas breakfast," she announced. "You and Sir Jeffery can help set the table. Okay?"

"Sure," replied Brian as he wiped the kiss off his cheek with the back of his hand. He bent over and whispered to his dog, "Next Christmas we'll go back for those golden nuggets. And you can help me find them for sure."

Sir Jeffery proudly held his head high, barked, wagged his tail, then strutted around the Christmas tree, the bright yellow dog glasses balanced beautifully on his ears and wet nose. He couldn't wait until next Christmas!